Crimson Fox: Jungle Warrior

Josh Zimmer

DEDICATION

Dedicated to foxes, they are cute, and have soft and fluffy fur!

The short story is inspired by various adventure elements in the jungle. The jungle is an wonderful adventure area to explore, because the character doesn't know what dangers or animals that they will encounter!

CONTENTS

ACKNOWLEDGMENTS

Foxes- For inspiring the story with their characteristics

Jungle Wilderness- for being an interesting story location to explore

The short story will teach readers how to be brave and courageous, when they are challenged to rescue someone in an dangerous environment!

CRIMSON FOX'S JOURNEY

In the jungle wilderness of Sunshine Paradise, there lived an family of foxes! Crimson was the son, and he had two parents, that were named Emily and Sam. The foxes were living an wonderful life, until they heard some rustling in the bush. Emily and Sam went to the bush to check it out. An group of raccoons ambushed them! Karson, the raccoon leader grabbed Emily by the neck, as she struggled in his grip. Sam jumped in to action and bit Karson's tail. Karson screamed in pain, and swats Sam away with his paw. Sam smashed in to an tree! Karson sharpens his claws, and whacked Emily on the head, knocking her out. The raccoon bandits tied up Sam and Emily, and threw them in to Karson's bag. Karson picked up the bag, and carried them to his hideout, with the raccoon bandits following behind him. Crimson was terrified, as he hides in his house, covering himself with his paws and tail. Crimson fell asleep, and used his tail as a pillow. The sun rose on an brand new day in the jungle. Crimson yawned and rubbed his eyes. Crimson got up, and stretched his paws. Crimson walked to the berry bush, and ate some berries for breakfast. He walked to his favorite rock, and did some pushups on the ground. He swung on the vines, and flipped in the air. Crimson walked through the jungle, and the wind blew through his fur. While walking through the jungle, he was admiring the plants and bugs, because they were amazing to look at. There was rustling in the bush! Crimson growled as he walked towards the bush, with his claws sharpened. Crimson walked to the bush, and there was an terrified raccoon named Paul. Paul said while trembling, "Don't hurt me, my fur is chewy!" Crimson put his paw on Paul's chest, as he continued growling! Crimson said, "Where did your leader take my parents!" Paul said, "He took them to the crocodile's lair." Crimson said, "Thanks for the tip!" He stabs his claws through the raccoon's chest, splattering blood everywhere, as Paul's dead body laid on the ground. Crimson continued walking through the jungle. The jungle was nice and calm, with the birds singing and the leaves moving in the wind. Crimson stopped at the pond, and drank some water to rehydrate his body. Crimson continued walking through the jungle! The air started to get mucky, and the trees started to change! Crimson knew that he was getting closer to the crocodile's lair, where his parents were held captive. Crimson swung on an vine to get himself over an fallen log. Crimson flipped in the air, and landed on his paws. Crimson walked through the jungle, admiring the different bugs and plants. Crimson saw an mucky pond, filled with muddy water and crocodiles, while he was walking through the jungle! He walked closer to the pond to check out the crocodile's foot prints. The foot prints were going in an certain direction! Crimson followed the footprints! An crocodile jumped out of the water and pounced on Crimson. Crimson growled and swatted the crocodile in the face. Crimson sharpened his claws, and grabbed the crocodile by the neck. Crimson stabs his paw through the crocodile's chest, and the crocodile laid on the ground. Crimson brushed the dirt off of his fur with his paw, as he continued following the footprints. Crimson noticed that he was getting close to an huge castle, guarded by crocodiles. He slowly walked to it, thinking that this must be the place where his parents have been kidnapped. An barricade of crocodiles swarmed Crimson, as he got closer to the castle. Crimson growled, as the crocodiles got closer to him. One of the crocodiles swung its tail at Crimson. Crimson dodged, and grabbed the crocodile's tail.

Crimson swung the crocodile around the area, hitting his other crocodile buddies in to the pond. Crimson threw the crocodile in to the air, and stabbed his claws through its chest. The crocodile laid on the ground in an puddle of blood. Crimson was determined to rescue his parents, as he walked closer to the castle. Crimson walked in to the castle, and he got swarmed by crocodiles. The crocodile leader, Matt, walked toward Crimson and said, "Who trespasses in our castle without permission?" Crimson growled and said, "I am here to rescue my parents! The raccoon bandits took them here, and I followed their paw prints to your castle." Matt said, "If you want your parents back, you have to go through us." The crocodile leader raised his flag, and sent his crocodile troopers after Crimson. The crocodiles swarmed Crimson! Crimson growled, and grabbed an crocodile's tail, swinging him around, and knocking the other troopers down. Crimson pounced on each crocodile with his claws sharpened, as he sped towards Matt. Crimson tackled Matt in to the ground. Crimson stabbed his claws through Matt's neck, as blood splattered out of his body. Crimson growled and said, "Give me my parents back, you monster! Crimson picks up Matt with his paw, and stabs his claws through Matt's chest. Blood splattered, as Crimson dropped Matt on the ground. Matt's body laid on the ground, as Crimson walked further in to the castle. Crimson walked in to the castle's kitchen! Karson, the raccoon leader, was dropping Crimson's parents in to the shark tank! Karson stopped, when he saw Crimson walk in. Crimson growled and said, "Drop my parents, I am here to rescue them." Karson said, "Perfect timing, little fox, you can join my meal, when I am done with you!" Karson dropped Sam and Emily on the ground! Karson tackled Crimson in to the ground! Karson tried to scratch Crimson's face, but Crimson swats him away with his paw. Crimson sharpens his claws, and scratches Karson's neck. Karson screams in pain, as he slides backwards. Crimson kicks Karson in the chest. Karson slides backwards in to the shark tank. Crimson sped towards Karson and grabbed him by the neck. Crimson smashed Karson in to the ground. Crimson sharpened his claws and stabbed them through Karson's neck. Blood splattered on to the ground. Crimson picked up Karson with his paw, and stabbed his claws through Karson's chest! Karson's body laid on the ground. Crimson walked toward Sam and

Emily, and untied them. Crimson said, "Mom and Dad, you are safe!" Crimson hugged Sam and Emily! Sam and Emily hugged Crimson back! Sam and Emily said, "You are an brave fox, I am glad that you rescued us." Crimson walked out of the crocodile's castle with Sam and Emily, as the sun sets.

ABOUT THE AUTHOR

Josh Zimmer is an crazy individual with an extreme imagination. He loves to have fun by listening to music, writing stories, and playing video games of various genres such as platforming, multiplayer online games, role playing games, and sports games. His favorite technology brands are Nintendo and Microsoft. They are wonderful role models for the industry. He commands an army of cats to his will with hugs, love, and snacks. He makes the cats purr and meow with happiness.

Crimson Fox: Jungle Warrior

Josh Zimmer

Crimson Fox: Jungle Warrior

Josh Zimmer

Crimson Fox: Jungle Warrior

Josh Zimmer

Crimson Fox: Jungle Warrior

Josh Zimmer

Crimson Fox: Jungle Warrior

Josh Zimmer

Crimson Fox: Jungle Warrior

Josh Zimmer

Crimson Fox: Jungle Warrior

Josh Zimmer

Crimson Fox: Jungle Warrior

Josh Zimmer

www.ingramcontent.com/pod-product-compliance
Lightning Source LLC
Chambersburg PA
CBHW072305130726
47910CB00012B/2534